This item is due for renewal or return to any of Fife's public libraries, on or before the latest date shown above. Renewals may be made in person, by phone or via our website

www.libcat.fife.gov.uk/TalisPrism

Tales from Whispery Wood

Make friends with the animals of Whispery Wood!

Be sure to read:

Mole's Useful Day

Flying Friends

... and lots, lots more!

Owl's Big Mistake

Julia Jarman
illustrated by Guy Parker-Rees

SCHOLASTIC

To Sam and Theo – J.J.

Scholastic Children's Books,
Commonwealth House, 1-19 New Oxford Street,
London, WC1A 1NU, UK
a division of Scholastic Ltd
London ~ New York ~ Toronto ~ Sydney ~ Auckland
Mexico City ~ New Delhi ~ Hong Kong

First published by Scholastic Ltd, 2002

ISBN 0 439 98103 4

Printed and bound by Oriental Press, Dubai, UAE

10 9 8 7 6 5 4 3 2 1

"Out of the … way!"
squeaked the voice again.

Rabbit was puzzled.
Who was squeaking?

He looked all around.
"Why?" he said. "And where? And who?"

"Because you're sitting on my head!"
squeaked the voice.

Rabbit hopped
to one side.

There, near a
leaf, was a small
brown creature.

"Thank you," it said. "I was under your
bottom, and – to answer your third
question – I'm Glow Worm."

The creature held out a leg. "Pleased to
meet you, Rabbit."

Rabbit shook the leg and stared.

"Pleased to meet you, er, Glow Worm. Welcome to Whispery Wood." Rabbit tried not to stare, but the creature didn't glow and it didn't look like a worm. It had legs and feelers, and a hard body, not a soft wiggly one.

"What were you doing down there?" Rabbit asked.

"Practising," said the creature.

Rabbit was still puzzled.

"Practising squirming," Glow Worm explained. She pointed at a group of earthworms, giggling nearby.

"Look at them laughing at me. Worms squirm, you see, but I can't – yet. Watch, can you, and tell me what I'm doing wrong."

The creature stuck its head in the earth and scrabbled its legs.

The worms giggled and squiggled so much, they nearly tied themselves into knots.

Rabbit looked at the worms.

Then he looked at Glow Worm and said,
"Er. Excuse me, I don't want to be rude,
but are you sure you're a worm?"

"Of course I'm sure!"
cried Glow Worm.
"I've got a
certificate to
prove it."

"A stiffy cat?"
said Rabbit.
"What's that?"

"A cert-if-i-cate," said Glow Worm. "A birth certificate. Look. It says what I am here." She pointed to the words. "See. Glow Worm. Female. I'm a girl."

On the certificate:

Birth
Certificate
Glow Worm
Female

Rabbit peered at the certificate, but he wasn't very good at reading small writing.

"Perhaps you read it wrongly," he said. "Perhaps you're a something else. I read things wrongly sometimes. Why don't we ask Owl? He's good at reading! We can ask him when he wakes up."

"Didn't, didn't read it wrong," said Glow Worm, looking cross.

But Rabbit didn't hear. He was still talking about Owl.

"He's ever so wise. You can ask him ever such hard questions like how to spell 'because'. If I don't know something I always ask Owl. All the Whispery Wood animals do."

Rabbit smiled at Glow Worm. "Don't worry. If he doesn't know what you are straight away, he'll sit on his thinking branch and think about it till he does."

Chapter Two

Rabbit was right. Owl was famous for being wise.

As soon as it got dark, Rabbit called up to him. "Owl, we've got a problem! Can you come and help, please?"

Owl flew down.
Zoom!

"Good evening, Rabbit! What's the problem?"

Rabbit pointed to Glow Worm. "It's not me, it's my new friend. Can you tell her what she is, please? She's a bit muddled."

"I'm not," said Glow Worm. "I just want to know how to squirm, that's all – and glow."

But Owl wasn't listening. He was busy counting.

"Six legs, two feelers," he said at last. "You're a beetle. Welcome to Whispery Wood, Beetle."

"There," said Rabbit, "you must have read it wrong."

"Didn't," said Glow Worm, stamping her feet. "Didn't, didn't, didn't!"

"Read what wrong?" said Owl.

"Her stiffy cat," said Rabbit.

"*Cert-if-i-cate*," said Glow Worm, glowering.

"A certificate?" said Owl. "May I see? Certificates are important."

Owl read it carefully, then asked, "Are you sure this is yours?"

"Yes," said Glow Worm.

"Well then, I must apologize," said Owl looking ruffled. "You are Glow Worm, a girl glow worm. I made a m-mistake."

"Why doesn't she glow then?" said Rabbit.

"And why can't I squirm?" said Glow Worm.

"I don't know," said Owl, flying up to his thinking branch, "but it's probably a phase you're going through. I need to think. I'll tell you in a minute."

But Owl didn't come down in a minute. He stayed on his thinking branch.

When Bat woke up, Owl wouldn't go flying with him as usual.

He said, "Sorry, Bat. Not now. I'm thinking."

Bat flew round Whispery Wood three times.

"Are you ready now, Owl? The moon's up. It's a great night for flying!"

"Sorry, no," said Owl. "I'm still thinking."

Owl was worried. His head was full of questions and he couldn't answer any of them.

Why doesn't Glow Worm glow?

Why can't she squirm?

Why has she got legs?

Down below, he heard Rabbit say, "Don't worry, Glow Worm. Owl will have the answers soon. Let's go visiting while we're waiting. The other animals might be able to help. Mole likes to be helpful."

Chapter Three

Mole was very pleased to be asked.

"Digging lessons! That's what you need!"
She began to dig with her big shovel paws.

"The other worms will stop laughing
when you're underground. Now, best foot –
er, feet – forward," she said. "Like this!"

Soon Mole was underground. "Come on!
See how you like it," she called out.

Glow Worm didn't like it – it was dark and
dirty underground – but she did like Mole.

"Mole's so friendly," Glow Worm said
to Rabbit.

"We're all friendly in Whispery Wood,"
said Rabbit.

Hedgehog was friendly too. He tried to help Glow Worm glow.

"I've got a collection of shiny bits," he said. "Magpie gave me some of them. I stick them to my spikes sometimes, for parties and things. You could stick them to your feet."

Rabbit and Hedgehog helped
Glow Worm stick on the shiny bits.

Then slowly – very slowly – they made
their way back to the old oak tree.

By the time they got back it was nearly morning. Bat was hanging from a branch waiting for them.

"I'm worried about Owl," he said. "He's in his hole and he won't come out. He's ashamed because he mistook Glow Worm for a beetle."

Rabbit said, "Poor Owl. Anyone can make a mistake. That's what he tells us. Tell him it doesn't matter."

Bat flew into the tree hole, where Owl
was sitting in the dark, talking to himself.
"I told her she was a beetle,"
Owl muttered.

Bat said, "Cheer up, Owl. Anyone can
make a mistake."

"But I'm not anyone, Bat!" Owl looked
very upset. "I am Wise Owl, famous for
being wise," he went on. "Well, I was, but
not any more."

Just at that moment some rooks flew over.
"Can you hear them?" said Owl. "Saying,
'Can't! Can't!' It's because I can't answer
the questions."

Bat put one of his big leathery wings round Owl.

"Owl, my friend, they were saying 'Caw! Caw!' like they always do."

But Owl shook his head. "They're telling everyone I'm useless," he said, "and they're right."

Chapter Four

Bat flew down to the others.

"We've got to do something quickly! We've got to make Owl feel better!"

"What can we do?" said Rabbit.

"I wish I could do something," said Glow Worm. "It's all my fault."

"No it's not," said Bat firmly.

"Don't worry," said Squirrel. "I'll take him some nuts."

"Good idea," said Bat. "I'll come too."

Bat flew up to Owl's hole. "Owl, I've come to tell you that we all like you very much."

Then Squirrel arrived with his nuts – and a flower from Mole.

"And we all miss you very much, too," said Squirrel.

But Owl wouldn't come out of his hole.

They left the presents in the entrance.

Squirrel said, "Maybe they'll cheer him up later."

The days went by. Every evening, the animals met at the bottom of the old oak tree. Bat and Squirrel went up to see Owl, but he wouldn't come out of his hole. And he wouldn't eat or drink.

One evening his feathers started to fall out.

"What's happening?" cried Rabbit as a feather landed in front of him.

"Owl's losing his face," said Bat. "What are we going to do?"

Then Bat saw something that made him forget Owl for a moment – a yellow-green light darting from tree to tree.

"What's that?" said Rabbit.

"I'm not sure," said Bat, whizzing off.

"But I'm going to find out!"

Then Rabbit saw another yellow-green light – on the ground! It was coming towards him, racing towards him.

"Look at me!" cried a tiny squeaky voice that Rabbit knew well. "And tell Owl!"

It was Glow Worm – glowing!

"It just happened!" she said breathlessly, as she arrived at Rabbit's burrow. "Owl was right. Being dull was just a phase."

Then she saw the darting yellow-green light up above. Suddenly her tail curled up and glowed even brighter.

Bat called down. "It's another Glow
Worm – and it's got wings!"

Rabbit called up, "Tell Owl! Tell Owl!"

Bat zoomed into
Owl's hole.

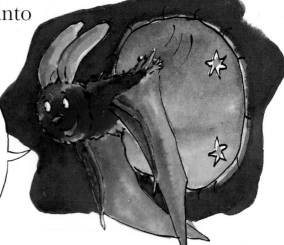

You were right!
You were right!
Glow Worm's glow
was out of sight.
But now she's shining!
Brightening up
the night!

"Owl! Owl, where are you?"

Owl wasn't there! His hole was empty!

Bat whizzed down to Rabbit – where the two glow worms were gazing into each other's eyes.

"Love at first sight," said Rabbit.

"Never mind that! Owl isn't there!" squeaked Bat. "He's left Whispery Wood!"

"Oh dear," said Rabbit. "Where can he be? What can we do?"

Suddenly Squirrel pointed to the starry sky. "Look, isn't that Owl?"

"Yes," said Bat.

"Yes, yes!" said Rabbit. "Hooray!"

"Owl! Owl!" they all yelled. "Come down! Glow Worm's glowing!"

Owl flew down.

"No need to shout," he said, sounding like the Owl they all knew.

"I've just been to the library, to check a few facts."

He looked at the glow worms and his voice dropped to a confident whisper.

"We are watching two glow worms, called worms because they are worms when babies. In their adult form, they are, as I said, beetles. The male has wings. The female doesn't. They both glow, but only in the mating season."

Suddenly Mole appeared. "What's all the noise about?"

"Sssh," said Rabbit. "It's Glow Worm. She's in love."

"In a glove?" said Mole. "I can't see a glove."
"In love," said Owl.
"Oh, sorry," said Mole.

"That's all right," said Owl, "anyone can make a mistake."

"Anyone?" said Rabbit.

"Anyone," said Owl, and all the animals clapped – quietly.